Katy and the Nurgla

HARRY SECOMBE

Illustrated by Priscilla Lamont

PUFFIN BOOKS

For Katy

Puffin Books, Penguin Books Ltd, Harmondsworth,
Middlesex, England
Penguin Books, 625 Madison Avenue,
New York, New York 10022, U.S.A.
Penguin Books Australia Ltd, Ringwood,
Victoria, Australia
Penguin Books Canada Ltd, 2801 John Street,
Markham, Ontario, Canada L3R 1B4
Penguin Books (N.Z.) Ltd, 182–190 Wairau Road,
Auckland 10, New Zealand

First published by Robson Books 1978
Published in Puffin Books 1980

Copyright © Harry Secombe, 1978
Illustrations copyright © Priscilla Lamont, 1978, 1980
All rights reserved

Made and printed in Great Britain by
Richard Clay (The Chaucer Press) Ltd,
Bungay, Suffolk

Set in 16 on 20 point Baskerville by
Filmtype Services Limited, Scarborough

It was one of those February days on the
Spanish island of Majorca when it was
neither bright nor dull. Since there did
not seem to be an exact word to describe
it, Katy made up her own. It was, she
decided, a 'brull' day – or possibly even
a 'dight' day. She was on a week's
holiday, although it was school-time,
because it was the only week in the
whole year that her mother and father

could get away together, and they could
hardly leave her behind. Katy was
delighted to have special permission to
be away from school; somehow it made
her feel rather important.

PUFFIN BOOKS

KATY AND THE NURGLA

Katy was on holiday in Majorca, and because it was term-time she had the whole beach to herself – until an old, tired monster swam up to the very rocks where she was sitting reading.

The Nurgla was cross, he was hideous, he was dreadfully wicked, but Katy just smiled and waved when she saw him, and in no time at all he was toiling up and down the beach to fetch her stones and seaweed for her games of make-believe!

After that, Katy and the Nurgla played together every day – watched eagerly from a spaceship above by the only beings who understood that the poor, cross Nurgla's future depended on this, the very first friendship of his life.

Harry Secombe's first book for children has all the best ingredients in just the right proportions: a monster, a spaceship, adventure, humour and more than a touch of happy sadness.

So here she was on the rocky north coast of Majorca, with no sign of the hordes of holiday-makers who crowded the beaches during the summer months. She had the entire place to herself.

Her father had unfortunately fallen down the steps of the plane and twisted his ankle when they arrived, and was finding it very painful to walk.

'A fine start to our holiday,' grumbled her mother as they breakfasted in their hotel room the next morning.

'Never mind,' said Katy, who was a Brownie with three badges and a smart salute. 'Don't worry about me, I'll find plenty to do. You look after Daddy. I think I'll go and play on the beach somewhere.'

'Now, do be careful,' said her mother.

'Yes, do – oh dear, my ankle,' groaned her father, who sometimes enjoyed a bit of bad health and being looked after.

The cook at 'El Hotel' where they were staying packed some sandwiches and an apple and a bottle of lemonade for Katy, and she put them into her little

beach bag along with her book. She said good-bye to her parents and promised to be back by tea-time.

As she made her way down towards a sheltered little bay hidden in the pine trees, another figure was heading for the same place – and no two creatures could have been more different.

The Nurgla was very, very old, and very, very tired, and he looked as old and as tired as he felt. His small head was wrinkled and lined with age; the two leathery horns which sprouted from the top of his forehead were crumpled and creased; and an untidy fringe of green, seaweed-like hair hung over his eyebrows and sometimes made him furious because it got into his eyes. Two large nostrils flared in the folds of his craggy cheeks, and dreadful sharp teeth jutted out from his huge jaws. A ridge of jagged spikes ran the length of the Nurgla's long, long neck, down the spine of his enormous body, right to the very tip of his scaly tail. To complete the horrible picture, his round body was covered in hard, overlapping, armour-like plates, and his vast flippers were an unbelievable size eighteen. In short, the Nurgla was hideous.

He had frightened people out of their wits since the beginning of time – and to

be perfectly honest, he enjoyed his fear-
some reputation. It made him feel
strong and powerful when people ran
from him in terror. Every summer he
spent his holidays in a lake in Scotland,
and whenever he rose from the water to

browse along the shore where his favourite weeds grew, thick and luscious, his dreadful appearance spread fear throughout the length and breadth of the land. Indeed, who has not heard of the Loch Ness Monster – the name that was given to the frightful creature that mysteriously appeared from time to time, and just as mysteriously disappeared?

Now, as he swam towards the little Majorcan bay where for hundreds of years he had spent a week or so every February, he was looking forward to a good rest and a nice quiet scratch on his favourite rocks. Paddling into shore, with just his eyes and nostrils showing above the waves, he suddenly saw that a small human creature was sitting on the very rocks where he liked to go. The Nurgla was furious. Stiff with rage, he

reared his terrible head out of the water
and roared. Flames streamed from his
gaping mouth.

Katy, who was busy reading a book
about Queen Elizabeth the First of
England, looked up at the noise. She saw
the monster, smiled at him, and waved.

'Hello!' she cried in a friendly way,
not at all frightened because she had
imagined far worse-looking creatures
than the Nurgla. In any case, at that
moment her book was much more in-

teresting than any old sea monster, and she went back to reading it.

The Nurgla swam closer in to the beach and roared again. This time the effort of belching forth flames made him cough, and two little puffs of black smoke drifted from his wide green nostrils and floated above his head like a comma and a full stop.

Katy put down her book and clapped her hands in delight. 'That's very clever,' she said.

Puzzled, the Nurgla rested his head on a nearby rock. Never before had his roars and his flames and his clouds of smoke had so little effect. Why, less than four hundred years ago, during a bout of indigestion in Queen Elizabeth the First's reign, he had sunk the Armada – a whole fleet of Spanish warships – in the English Channel! Unfortunately, he remembered bitterly, the weather had been so bad at the time that his part in the affair had been hidden by the mist, and some fellow called Sir Francis Drake had got all the credit for sinking the Armada. The Nurgla snorted at the unfairness of it all, and another little cloud of smoke rose like a full stop into the air.

'Now you're being silly,' said Katy. 'You can't have two full stops in the same sentence.' She picked up her book again and ignored the monster.

The Nurgla felt all his billion years of existence suddenly pressing on him like a lead weight. Crushed and exhausted, he heaved a great shuddering sigh which riffled the pages of Katy's book and rattled the teacups in 'El Hotel' up on the cliff.

'Oh, all right,' said Katy. 'If you're sorry, I'll forgive you.' She pointed to a small seaweed-covered boulder. 'Bring me that rock over there and we'll play a game of building a house.'

Speechless with amazement, the monster who was feared all over the seven seas and at least three oceans found himself fetching and carrying

stones in his mouth and placing them on the beach as Katy ordered.

'That's right. We'll have the kitchen just here. Pick up that knobbly stone by your tail – we'll use that for the gas stove, and we'll have that piece of seaweed as a carpet for the dining-room.'

Up and down the deserted beach the Nurgla toiled, collecting shells and sea-weed, moving boulders, and arranging them like the walls of a house. Soon, in spite of himself, he began to like playing this game. It was quite a change to be told what to do.

Just when he was working up a fine sweat from the first honest day's work he had ever done, Katy suddenly said, 'Oh, dear, I'd better be getting back. I promised my mother and father I would be home when the sun went down as far as that hill over there. I haven't got a watch, you see.' She picked up her beach bag. 'Bye-bye,' she said, then stopped and scratched her head. 'What shall I call you? I know – I'll call you Fred, because that's the name of my old teddy bear, and you're like him in a way, even though you are all green and wet and a little bit ugly.' Katy turned and started to walk away up the beach.

19

Behind her, the Nurgla shook his head in disbelief. The spell of the pleasant afternoon was wearing off, and his temper got the better of him. 'Ugly?' he snorted to himself. 'I won't be spoken to like that. Doesn't she realize who I am? Why, I've eaten things like her before breakfast!' And he opened his monstrous mouth and began to slither after the little girl.

Hearing the pebbles rattling behind her, Katy swung round and saw the Nurgla with his mouth gaping wide. 'I see,' she said. 'You're hungry.' She reached into her beach bag and took out an apple, which she tossed into the huge open jaws. 'That's for being a good sport and helping me build a house. If you'd like to play again tomorrow, I'll see you here at the same time. I'm on holiday until Saturday.'

She walked off, leaving the Nurgla still open-mouthed in astonishment. As she reached the foot of the cliff, she looked back. 'Don't eat with your mouth open,' she called, wagging her finger. 'Mummy says it's not nice.'

The monster's terrible teeth clamped together.

'That's better,' Katy smiled, and waved him good-bye.

When she got back to the hotel her mother said, 'Did you have a lovely time, Katy?'

'Yes thanks,' said Katy, taking off her coat and throwing her beach bag on the floor. 'I've been playing with a sea monster.'

'That's nice,' said her mother, picking up the bag from the floor and putting it away in a cupboard. 'Better go and wash your hands, then, before we have supper.'

'What an imagination that child has,' murmured her father, who was resting his foot on the bed and holding a glass of whisky in his hand.

'So have you if you think that whisky is good for sprained ankles,' retorted Katy's mother, with a little sniff.

Meanwhile, a hundred miles above the earth hovered a shimmering, cigar-shaped spaceship. Its crew had been watching Katy's meeting with the Nurgla on a large television screen. The

space-creatures were very unusual and rather beautiful in appearance: each looked like a blob of different-coloured light – orange, pink, green, yellow, purple, amber, silver – every colour imaginable. And they had one remarkable power: they could understand each other's thoughts and read what was going on in each other's minds, so there was no need for them to speak to one another. They only had to think.

One blob of red light, larger than all the others, thought to the rest of the crew, 'It could be that this meeting with the small human is the Nurgla's last chance to make up for his bad behaviour in the past.'

The smallest blob, a blue one, was puzzled. 'What do you mean? And who is the Nurgla?'

'From the first day he was created –

when he was just a tiny pinprick of light – the Nurgla was always getting into trouble of some sort,' explained Big Red Blob in thought. 'Not really *bad* trouble – to tell the truth, he was more of a mischievous blob than a wicked one. He liked to play practical jokes such as creeping up on others and exploding behind them with a big bang.'

Little Blue Blob thought a chuckle.

Big Red Blob went even redder with annoyance.

Little Blue Blob blushed bluely. 'Sorry,' he thought.

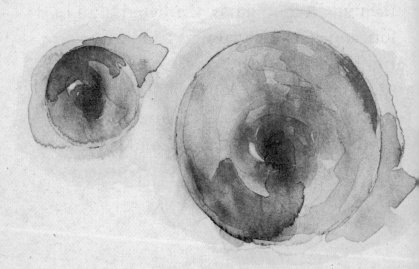

'Mind you,' continued Big Red Blob, 'he was only five hundred years old, so we used to make allowances for him. Later on he became one of the Shining Ones like ourselves – special blobs who are trained to undertake all the most dangerous tasks in space. He did very well – for a time.'

The other blobs flickered on and off in agreement.

'Well? What happened then?' Little Blue Blob was impatient to know the whole story.

Big Red Blob grew even bigger and the multicoloured crew gathered round, forming a bright circle of light like a rainbow. 'A billion years ago, one of our spaceships landed on Earth to find out whether it would make a suitable home for the Shining Ones. I was among those who were sent out to explore. In order to survive the Earth's climate, we had to put on the shapes of the animals which roamed the Earth at that time – dinosaurs, they were called, clumsy great creatures. Now that we no longer need to look for new worlds in which to live, most blobs have lost the knack of changing themselves at will into different shapes.' Big Red Blob paused for a moment. 'I wonder if I can still do it?'

A gigantic, reptile-like creature covered with armour plating and standing on two mighty legs suddenly filled the spaceship. The other blobs went pale with fright. Then, just as quickly as it had appeared, the creature turned into another, even more frightening, monster, and then another. Six awful-looking creatures followed one another in rapid succession. Then they were all gone, and Big Red Blob reappeared.

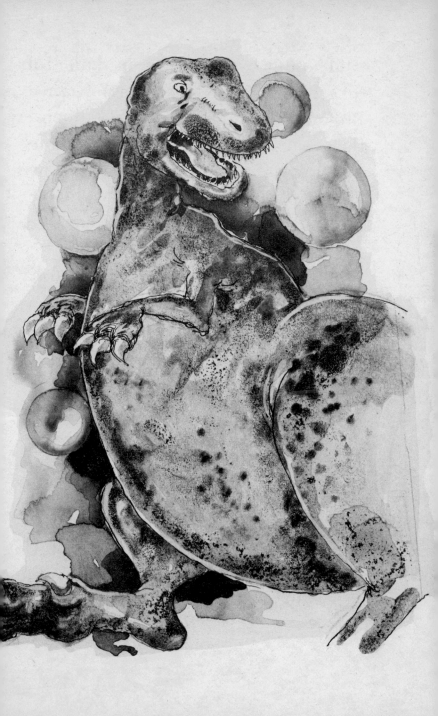

'Those were all different kinds of dinosaur – a Tyrannosaurus Rex, a Brontosaurus, a Pterodactyl, and so on – they were the sorts of shapes we had to put on,' he thought to the others by way of explanation. 'Whew – I haven't done that sort of thing for a million years or more. I'm pleased I can still do it.'

The other blobs recovered from their fright and congratulated their leader on this amazing performance.

'Thank you. Anyway, the Nurgla – he was always the odd one out – chose to

become a Plesiosaurus, a sea-animal. Not satisfied with that, he thought it would be fun to give himself the ability to breathe out flames and smoke.' Big Red Blob thought a sigh, and quivered. 'The Supreme Brightness had ordered us to return to the spaceship after two weeks with our reports, and warned us that if we were late we would be left behind on Earth, unable to change back out of the dinosaur shapes we had put on.'

The crew changed colour ten times at the horror of the thought.

'Everyone arrived back at the ship in plenty of time, clanking and clattering in their great clumsy animal bodies – everyone, that is, except the Nurgla.' Big Red Blob went a deeper red, and the colours of the crew's lights deepened, too. 'It seems that somewhere off the coast of Siberia he asked a real Plesiosaurus the way to the North Pole and when he got no reply – and of course he wouldn't because the brain of a real Plesiosaurus was only the size of a pea and it couldn't understand a word – the Nurgla lost his temper and splashed it with his tail. The Earth creature grew angry, there was a terrible fight, and the Nurgla actually made its nose bleed.'

The crew's lights blacked out for two seconds as they pictured the monstrous deed.

'Yes,' thought on Big Red Blob sadly.

'The very worst thing a member of our race, the Shining Ones, can do is to hurt another creature in any way what-soever. And to cause one to bleed is quite unforgivable! The Supreme Brightness ordered that the Nurgla should be taught a lesson: he was to be left behind on Earth until he had made up for wounding a fellow-creature and being a bad blob. When he heard this, the Nurgla stormed off in a huff without waiting to hear what he had to do in order to be allowed to return to us. So he never knew the four things that had to happen before he could be forgiven. Firstly, he had to do an honest day's work and be paid for it; secondly, he had to feel the touch of a human hand in affection; thirdly, he had to love and be loved in return; and finally he had to shed a tear – not because he was sorry for himself, but a genuine tear. Every thousand years we return to Earth to observe the Nurgla's behaviour, but time is short now and we shall not be back again until after the Nurgla is dead.'

The other blobs grew sad and their lights dimmed.

'I'm afraid that there is little hope of him returning to us now. So far he has done all the wrong things and has terrified human beings and animals alike. Just look at this.'

Big Red Blob thought hard, and a list of the Nurgla's wrong-doings appeared in the air before them. It was a very long list of hundreds of naughty deeds.

'See there – a certain Saint George severely wounded him for carrying off a beautiful maiden. The Nurgla was lucky to get away alive – Saint George actually boasted that he had killed him.

And look at all those earthquakes and tidal waves the Nurgla caused by flame-throwing under water . . . Then there was the Spanish Armada affair. *And* he frightened the crew of a ship called the *Marie Celeste* so much that they all jumped overboard, leaving the ship to sail on without them. I am afraid that this is his very last chance.'

Little Blue Blob left the ring of coloured light and came forward excitedly. 'There *is* some hope, though, this time! The Nurgla helped the small human creature, Katy, to build a make-believe house, and she gave him an apple in return. Surely that's the same as doing a job of work and being paid for it? If so, that is the first of the four conditions laid down by the Supreme Brightness.'

Big Red Blob brightened. 'Yes... ye-es, I suppose that might do. Perhaps this Katy *can* save the Nurgla, but there isn't much time. We can only stay in orbit here until Saturday. After that we must go – the Supreme Brightness has work for us in another universe.'

'I'd like some shrimp-paste sand-wiches as well, please,' said Katy to the cook at 'El Hotel' as he packed her lunch for another day on the beach.

'*Si,*' replied the cook, who didn't speak English.

'Mummy is going to have her hair done this afternoon and Daddy has twisted his ankle, so I'm going to play with Fred the sea monster in our little secret cove.'

The cook smiled and nodded even though he didn't understand a word. He liked the little girl with her rosy cheeks and bright eyes, and he patted her dark

curly head. He wondered why she wasn't fatter, with all the food she seemed to eat. She had already packed half a chicken, four apples, three bananas and a huge mound of cheese sandwiches into her beach bag. Now she seemed to want more. He raised his arms in the air and shook his head.

'Oh, all right,' said Katy. 'I expect there's enough there to keep Fred happy. Thank you very much.' She skipped out of the kitchen and headed for the little bay.

The Nurgla was already waiting, lurking behind some rocks, as she skidded down the pebbly beach.

'Sorry I'm late,' she called. 'I had to wait for our lunch to be prepared.' She put down her beach bag with a sigh of relief. 'Ooh! That's heavy.' She began to unpack the sandwiches.

The Nurgla poked his head out from his hiding place and sent a small tongue of flame darting from his mouth.

'What a good idea!' cried Katy. 'We can have toasted sandwiches.' She picked up a stick that had been washed ashore and was bleached white with the sea and the sun. 'Do that again with

your mouth.' She stuck some of the sandwiches on the end of the stick and held it out in front of her. 'Just a minute, let me get some of that hair out of your eyes.' Katy pushed the Nurgla's green seaweed hair to one side with her hand. 'There. Now you can see what you're doing. Breathe out slowly and I shall be able to toast the sandwiches on your fire. Not too much, mind, or you'll burn them.'

Obediently the Nurgla did as he was told, belching out a steady stream of flame.

'That's lovely. Careful – don't breathe out too hard. If I put the chicken just

behind your front teeth you can warm
that up at the same time.'

Very soon a delicious smell of roast chicken and toasted cheese sandwiches filled the beach, and Katy and the Nurgla sat down to their picnic. Katy ate only two sandwiches and an apple, leaving the rest for the Nurgla. She made him eat properly, placing the food in his terrible jaws, watching to see that he chewed it thoroughly, and scolding him when he made a noise. She had no idea that he had eaten a shoal of mackerel for breakfast that morning and was not the least bit hungry, and that he was forcing the sandwiches down out of politeness – which was something he had never done before in all his billion years.

Up in the spaceship the blobs were flashing on and off and changing colour madly.

'That's two things!' thought Little Blue Blob to Big Red Blob, triumphantly. 'The Nurgla had to be touched by a human hand in affection – and Katy moved his hair out of his eyes.'

'Ye-es,' thought Big Red Blob grudgingly. 'I think the Supreme Brightness will accept that.'

The whole spaceship glowed with colour as the crew's excitement mounted.

Down below, Katy was making the Nurgla clear up the beach by burning the litter with spurts of flame from his fiery mouth. When all was tidy, she sat down on the rocks near his head to read aloud to him.

'I think we'd better start off with *The Wind in the Willows*,' she said, looking through the books she had brought with her. 'A history book about Queen Elizabeth the First might be a bit too advanced for a sea monster.'

'If only she knew about me sinking the Spanish Armada,' thought the Nurgla, allowing himself a little smile. His jaw muscles, which hadn't been used for smiling for hundreds of years, creaked so loudly that Katy had to tell him to be quiet while she was reading.

And that's how it was every afternoon until Friday. Katy would take her beach bag full of food and her copy of *The Wind in the Willows* and race down to the beach. There she and Fred would play a game, and then he would put his dreadful head in her lap and she would stroke his awful green hair as she read aloud to him.

Katy's parents were glad that she was busy and happy and didn't ask too many questions. They seldom listened to her answers, anyway, because she was only a little girl.

Then on Friday, just as Katy was getting ready to go down to the beach, it began to rain. And not just a drizzling rain, but a downpour. The heavens opened and water got in everywhere, even into Katy's father's whisky as he sat near the window, looking out.

'You can't go out in this, Katy,' said her mother. 'We can't have you being ill with pneumonia or something when we get back home.'

'But I must, I *must*. I promised Fred that I would be there today. I'm on the last chapter of *The Wind in the Willows* and I've got to give him his lunch.'

Katy was in tears, but her mother was firm and sent her to bed, telling her that a day's rest wouldn't do her any harm.

'I think that child's sickening for something,' said her father. 'Look behind her ears for spots – it might be scarlet fever.'

'You mean measles. That's when you look for spots behind their ears.' Katy's mother sat and looked out at the rain. 'That's spoiled my game of golf this afternoon,' she said crossly.

At the cove the Nurgla waited, unaffected by the rain and becoming more impatient by the minute. 'Where is that girl?' he thought angrily. 'I want her to read to me. She's on the last chapter of

The Wind in the Willows and I want to know how it ends.'

He waited until it grew dark, and still Katy did not come. Furious, the Nurgla rushed out to sea and frightened a shipful of holiday-makers cruising near Gibraltar, but it did not make him feel any better. For once in his life he got no pleasure from seeing people's fear of him. Miserably, he went back to his cove – or rather, to *their* cove – his and Katy's cove – as he now thought of it, and lay quietly in the water, thinking.

In her bed at the hotel, Katy, who had cried herself to sleep after tea, woke

48

up and looked out of the window towards the place where she knew Fred
was waiting for her.

'I love you, Fred,' she whispered to
the dark night.

Up in the spaceship the blobs shim-
mered and glowed feverishly.

'Stop that flashing on and off,' Big
Red Blob thought sternly, and they all
burned steadily, trying to contain their
excitement.

'She loves him,' thought-whispered Little Blue Blob. 'Now if only the Nurgla . . .'

The Nurgla lay thoughtfully in the water and wondered what had come over him these past few days. He had met a little human creature, the only one he could ever remember who had not been frightened of him. Indeed, she had actually been kind to him and treated him like a friend. And he had enjoyed their meetings so much, he now realized, that for nearly a week he hadn't given a thought to being wicked and scaring people out of their wits. He did not know why she hadn't come to meet him, but he was sure of one thing: he missed her dreadfully. At last he arrived at the only possible conclusion.

'I love her! That's why I feel so strange – *I love Katy!*'

The spaceship crew were thrilled.

'That's the third condition – Katy loves him, and the Nurgla loves her in return,' thought Little Blue Blob, shining with happiness, and even Big Red Blob was glowing scarlet.

Saturday morning came, bright and sunny, but Katy's mother, busy packing in order to leave early to catch the plane, told her not to leave the hotel.

'Please, Mummy, *please* let me go and say good-bye to Fred. *Please*.'

'Don't be silly, Katy. All this talk about sea monsters and things. There isn't time. I'm going downstairs to fetch your father and then we'll have to get the taxi.'

Katy made up her mind. As soon as her mother had left the room, she went out into the corridor, climbed down the fire-escape and slipped out of the back door. She ran as fast as she could down to the beach, calling to Fred. The Nurgla rose from the rocks where he had been lying all night, and craned his head towards her in love.

Katy cradled his head in her arms and

sobbed. 'Oh, I'm sorry about yesterday but you see it was raining and Mummy wouldn't let me come out. I was so upset that I cried all night because I love you, Fred, and I shall miss you and I haven't even finished reading you *The Wind in the Willows.*' She put her wet rosy cheek next to the Nurgla's seamed, wrinkled face and rested it there.

Suddenly, something began to happen. Deep down in Fred's body a sob began to form. Up his long, long neck it came, and his red-rimmed eyes grew wet. He blinked to drive away the strangely upsetting feeling, but he could not hold back the tear. It rose in the corner of the eye next to Katy's cheek like water welling up from an underground spring, clean and clear and pure. The tear brimmed over and coursed slowly down the monster's cheek,

over the scaly lips, past the dreadful teeth, and dropped sizzling into the sea at Katy's feet.

'That's it!' thought Big Red Blob happily. 'He's fulfilled all four conditions – now he can leave his sea monster body and return to us. Beam the Nurgla aboard!'

The blobs went wild with delight as a new shining golden light came to join them. They crowded around it, dancing with joy, and forming one huge shifting kaleidoscope of light.

Katy could not believe her eyes. One minute Fred was there and the next he was gone. She lowered her empty arms and looked down at the water lapping around her ankles. She realized with surprise that she was wearing her shoes and socks ready for going home. As she turned to leave, she saw in a tiny patch of sand a most unusual pebble. It was shaped like a tear, and when she held it up to the light she found she could see through it. Katy turned it over in her hands. It felt curiously warm, and instantly comforted her for the sudden loss of her friend.

She heard shouts, and looking up saw her father standing at the top of the cliff, calling to her and waving his walking stick. When she reached him, the sadness in her eyes stopped him from scolding her.

'Come on, old girl,' he said, putting his arm round her shoulders and forgetting his bad ankle for a moment. 'Been saying good-bye to your old seamonster friend, eh?' He waved his stick in the air. 'Can't see him myself – must be shy, I suppose. Still, good-bye, Fred, wherever you are.'

'Good-bye, Fred,' thought Katy, clutching her pebble.

Her father took out his handkerchief. 'No good crying. Come on, have a good blow. There, that's better.'

'Will we be late for the plane?' Katy asked.

'No, we've just about got time – it leaves at two o'clock,' answered her father, thinking to himself regretfully that he would not have time to buy his whisky at the duty-free shop.

'You can usually buy it on the plane,' Katy said.

Her father stopped and stared at her. 'What?' he asked in surprise. 'What did you say?'

'I said, you can usually buy whisky on

the plane – if you don't have time to get any in the duty-free shop, I mean.'

'Good heavens, how did you know what I was thinking? Has Fred been teaching you mind-reading or something?'

Katy smiled to herself. She kissed the tear-shaped pebble and put it carefully into her pocket.

'Come on, Daddy,' she said, 'or we'll be late.'

Who is he?

His name is Smudge, and he's the mascot of the Junior Puffin Club.

What is that?

It's a Club for children between 4 and 8 who are beginning to discover and enjoy books for themselves.

How does it work?

On joining, members are sent a Club badge and Membership Card, a sheet of stickers, and their first copy of the magazine, *The Egg*, which is sent to them four times a year. As well as stories, pictures, puzzles and things to make, there are competitions to enter and, of course, news about new Puffins.

For details of cost and an application form, send a stamped addressed envelope to:

The Junior Puffin Club
Penguin Books Limited
Bath Road
Harmondsworth,
Middlesex UB7 0DA